POPEYE
The Movie Novel™

Edited and Adapted by
RICHARD J. ANOBILE

Based upon the Screenplay by
JULES FEIFFER

and the Film Directed by
ROBERT ALTMAN

AVON
PUBLISHERS OF BARD, CAMELOT AND DISCUS BOOKS

Anamorphic frame blowups
by Ryan Herz and Mark Henry

Interior Design: The Harry Chester Studio

Everything Is Food
by Harry Nilsson
Copyright © 1980 by Famous Music Corporation
Used by Permission

Everybody's Got To Eat
by Harry Nilsson
Copyright © 1980 by Famous Music Corporation
Used by Permission

He's Large
by Harry Nilsson
Copyright © 1980 by Famous Music Corporation
Used by Permission

I Yam What I Yam
by Harry Nilsson
Copyright © 1980 by Famous Music Corporation
Used by Permission

I'm Popeye The Sailor Man
by Sammy Lerner
Copyright © 1934 by Famous Music Corporation
Copyright renewed 1961 and assigned to Famous Music Corp.
Used by Permission

About the editor:

RICHARD J. ANOBILE is one of the foremost producers of
media-related books in the United States. He has edited
several in a film comedy series, including the best-selling
Why a Duck?

Anobile pioneered the use of the frame blow-up technique to re-create films in book form and the result, *The
Film Classics Library*, has been widely hailed in the U.S.
and Europe.

Other Anobile books include the international bestseller
The Marx Bros. Scrapbook (Groucho Marx, co-author), *Be-
yond Open Marriage* (Ulla Anobile, co-author), *Alien Movie
Novel*, *The Rocky Horror Picture Show Movie Novel* and
The Book of Fame.

Anobile studied at The City University of New York's In-
stitute of Film Technique. He now resides in Hollywood
where, in addition to broadening his work in publishing,
he is also developing various television and feature film
projects. His next project will be a Movie Novel of "Out-
land," a Ladd Co./Warner Bros. Release. Following that, he
will create two books about the forthcoming M-G-M film,
"The Clash of the Titans."

Acknowledgements:

I would like to take this opportunity to thank Robert Altman and
Lion's Gate Films for helping me make this book possible,
especially Tony Lombardo and his editorial group: John Bucklin,
Jack Holmes, David Simmons, Raja Gosnell, Bob Lederman, Paul
Rubell, Jacque Toberen, Steve Tucker, Ted Whitfield, Eric
Whitfield, Leslie Whitfield and Richard Whitfield.
Also, Bridget Terry and Rick Sparks.
Howard A. Levine of Paramount Pictures Corporation.
And, Kay Kildahl and Chris Berry.
RJA

Note:
This book was created prior to the final cut of the film.
Therefore, there will be differences between this Movie Novel
and the film in release. There may be sequences in the film not
in this book and sequences in this book not in the film. The order
of scenes may vary and some dialogue will be different from
that which you will hear in the theater.
RJA/August, 1980.

POPEYE

A brilliant sunrise buoys the spirit of a lone sailor in a battered dinghy as he braves a sudden squall in hopes of reaching the land he has sighted.

As the weary sailor enters the harbor, the town of Sweethaven is suddenly washed in sunlight.

Somewhat astonished, the sailor mutters, "I didn't see no Swee'having onna chart! Ten degrees starboard here, anudder twenty degrees starboard dere. Nasty Bend! Not no Swee'having! Dis should be Nasty Bend!"

"I never makes navigational errors! Now I'm over here, but I wuz over dere. An' den I sailed over dis way … "

"Oh, here ik is. Right here! Nasty Bend! Except ik ain't. Ik's Swee'having! Dey changed da name o' da town on me is wot dey done! Thassa good one on me! Erf, erf!"

"Can't fine a town if dey changes da name on ya, can ya? Swee'having is ik!"

"*Wreckhaving* is more like ik! So many wrecks out dere, I cudda walked da last knot. Erf, erf."

Spying someone in the town's crow's nest, the sailor shouts jubilantly, "Ahoy there!"

But the watchman doesn't seem to want to notice.

"Hmm, guess he didn't see me. Guess his eye sike ain't so good. He should eat carroks."

" 'Minds me o' da time four monts at sea onna *Saucy Mary*. Lost our groceries in a six day blow roundin' da Cape. Nuttin on board t'eat but carroks."

"After six weeks o' carroks, me eye sike got so good I cud see thru walls! See da fishes on the bottom o' da oceang."

"After ten weeks o' carroks, I cud see thru flesh — look a man thru t'his bare bones!"

"Ya can go too far wit a good t'ing. Even eye sike."

"You just dock?" asks the man.
"I has," says the sailor.

"I'm the Taxman and that'll be a twenty-five-cent Docking Tax. Where's your seacraft?"

"Ik ain't a seacraft, ik's me dinghy, and ik's under da wharf."

"This your goods?"
"Dey is."
"You're new in town, right?"
Under his breath the sailor mutters,
"Ya call dis a town!"
Then he shouts, "Yeah?"

"First of all there's a seventeen-cent New-In-Town Tax, forty-five cent Rowboat-Under-The-Wharf Tax, and a dollar Leaving-Your-Junk-Lying-Around-The-Dock Tax. All together you owe the Commodore a dollar-eighty-seven."

"What da ... ? Who is dis Commodore?"

"Is that in the nature of a question? If so, there is a nickel Question Tax."

"Oh, forget ik!" the disgusted sailor snaps. The Taxman continues, "And exact change, please. I'm an exact-change Taxman."

"Here's a dollar."

Their curiosity aroused by the appearance of the stranger, Sweethaven children watch as the sailor pays the tax, coin by coin.

"An' a quarter, eh, here's a dime ... "

"An' here's a penny ... "

Noticing the children, the Taxman shouts, "Look, kids! There's a five-cent Curiosity Tax!"

"Hey!" shouts the sailor.

"Hey, I'm tryin' t' pay me taxes!"

"Hmmm, dis tax,
dat tax.
Who's mad? Me?
I ain't mad.
I'm disgustipated
is all.
Not mad."

"Ik ain't my
town. I got
no right t'be
mad. I got
a right t'be
disgustipated.
Nobody fools
wit me right
t'be disgustipated.
Maybe dey got
a room for
renk here."

But Sweethaven seems short on hospitality.

"Oh, well!" mutters the sailor as a group of men struggle to move a piano. Each shouts in turn, "Got it? I got it. You got it?"

The sailor spies an old corncob pipe on the pavement.

"Nice lookin' pipe!"

One of the movers shouts, "Uh-oh, it's got me!"

As the piano begins to fall, another shouts, "I don't got it!"

And the preoccupied sailor remains unmindful of his predicament.

"Hmm, I ain't had a good pipe since da terrible Toar smacked a pipe down me t'roat so hard, fer six monts I wuz blowin' smoke outta me toenails!"

" 'At was a good fight. But I hated t' lose me pipe!" says the sailor as he's nudged by the swinging piano.

"Hey, you!"

Effortlessly, the sailor gives the piano a shove.

"Hey, who was that guy?" someone asks.

"Erf, erf."

As the sailor wanders through the town looking for lodging, he amuses himself with his own conversation. "Quiet little town. Not too pretty. Not too ugly."

"Cud be Fishtail where I had me fight to da finich wit Softie Coogan. T'ree-hunnerd pounds o' glop! We might still be fightin' 'cept Softie fell asleep onna terd day!"

"A bunch o' carroks."
"No carrots."

"You ain't got carroks! Wot are dose? Prunes?"
"Phooey on carrots! Take broccoli!"

"I yam inna mood fer carroks!"
"Phooey on carrots! Take spinach!"
"If I wanted spinach I wud axs fer spinach. I want carroks!"

"For you, carrots are a dollar."
"How come carroks issa dollar?"
"A dollar-fifty. You buy what I don't feel like selling, it costs two dollars!"

Reluctantly the sailor takes the carrots and tosses the vendor a coin.

"Hey, deadbeat!" shouts the vendor "You only gave me a quarter!"

"I pays wot I feels like paying!" announces the sailor as he leaves.

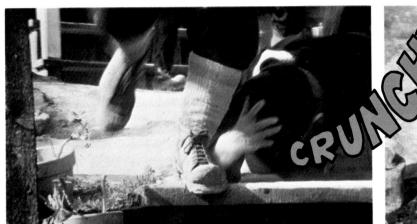

"Hey! What is dis?"

"Come on, come an' get ik!"

"Ah, pardon me! Are you the piano tuner or the man with the party favors?"

"You got a room fer renk?"

"What? For what?"

"Renk! Renk! Ya got a sign dat says ya got a room fer renk!"

"Oh, my stars and gardens! My mind was a million miles away. Come in before you catch your death of mud."

"Ah, me carroks."

"Well, good luck to you!"

"Hrmph!"

"I'm sorry, Mother, but it's ugly! I ask you, have you ever seen anything so ugly? I won't be engaged in this hat!"

"I heard that!" says Cole. "Don't think I didn't hear that!"

"She owes me an apology!"

"Ugly! There's
nothing left
to say.
What do you
think, Mother?"

"I think it's
up to you,
dear."

"It's ugly! I think it's a
conspiracy. Why would
they manufacture
deliberate ugliness unless
they wanted me to look
ugly? If we find that out,
we find out everything!"

"I can't get
engaged.
You'll have
to tell Bluto.
I can't."

"We have to cancel the
party tomorrow night.
It's not my fault that it's
ugly!"

"Uh-oh! What are you doing listening in on a private conversation between me and my mother? I've got a good mind to have my father call a policeman!"

"Ah, Olive, would you show Mr. ... er ... "
"Popeye."
" ... Mr. Eye the spare room?"

"Go upstairs, Mr. Eye.
Olive will show you your room."
"Ah, ik's Popeye," mutters the sailor.

"I don't see why I have to do anything on the day before my engagement party when nothing is ready, especially me!! And what kind of name is that? Popeye! Pret-ty strange!"

"Hmmm," groans Popeye under his breath, "Wot kinds of name is Olive Oyl? Some kinds of lubricant?"

"Ugly?" shouts Cole. "You owe me an apology!"
"What?" screeches Olive.

Popeye grumbles. "I wonder who stuck a feather you know where!"

"What did you say?"
"Er ... ah, hope this nice weather don't clear."

Olive struggles with the door.
"Your name really Olive?"
"So what?"

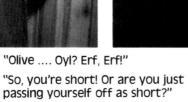

"Olive .... Oyl? Erf, Erf!"
"So, you're short! Or are you just passing yourself off as short?"

"Cud I see me room now?"
"As if I cared," says Olive as the jammed door suddenly gives way.

"It's a real nice lookin' room."

"Careful how you treat that bed! I'll have you know it belonged to my Uncle Crude Oyl, who got washed up in Weehawken. Nothing goes on this bed! And watch that lamp behind you!" shrieks Olive as she jumps across the bed towards the lamp.

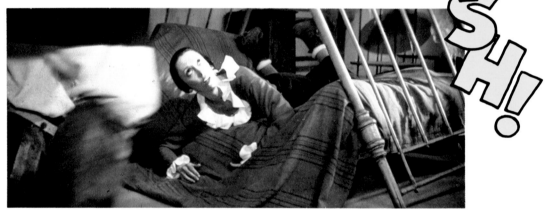

"Here, lets me
help ya."

"Thanks fer yer help, Miz Oyl!"

That evening:

"How do you like that!" says Cole to Castor and Geezil. "Gold is up twenty cents to two dollars an ounce!"

As Wimpy surveys the dinner table, Castor remarks, "Boy! Dad, I could have made a fortune in gold fillings if Bluto had let me go directly to the Commodore. But he's so jealous of me ... "

Nana interrupts.
"Who wouldn't be?"

"Me!" says Cole. "I'm not jealous of Castor! He's my son. A man jealous of his own son? You owe me an apology!"

"I didn't mean you," answers Nana.

"The Commodore is a paragon of sagacity," expounds Wimpy. "If I can ever put in a good word ... "

Geezil interrupts. "*Shut up* is a word! *Pass* is another word!"

"Oh, Mr. Eye!" announces Nana.

"Er, it's Popeye."

Olive goes
to her seat.

Nana
continues
undaunted.
"Have you met
Mr. Wimpy,
Mr. Geezil,
my son Castor,
my husband,
Cole."

"Oh, I can't find anything!" whimpers Olive.

"What are you looking for?" asks Nana.

"A glass!"

"Here's a glass."

But Olive continues.
"That's a short, fat, ugly glass!
I want a tall, pretty, slender glass!"

Nana is curt.
"They're all broken!"

"I could make a fortune in fish futures," says Castor.

"Fish? Fish futures smell!" remarks Geezil.

Olive fidgets. Nana notices.
"Now what do you want, Olive?"

"Not a thing. I don't want a thing!
A fork. I want a fork!"

"Right by your plate! If it was a knife, it would cut you."

"Will you sit down, Mr. Eye!" barks Nana.

Olive complains.
"And a knife! Why don't I have a knife? And a nice dress!!!"

Geezil groans, "Pass fish plizz."

Wimpy expands, "That's a good idea!
Fish, Miss Oyl. Fish! Fish before matrimony, Miss Oyl."

Olive whines, "Mother, he's picking on me!"

"Mr. Wimpy, you musn't talk Olive out of her engagement. Four times engaged is three times much!"

"You know, I've never let a girl of mine break my engagement. I'd break her nose before she'd break my engagement! And you'd better not pull on me what you pull on Bluto!"

"Don't be stupid! I can't get engaged to you. You're my brother!"

"Well, I don't know. Captain Bluto has the patience of Job. Or is that job? He's got a very good job. Why he runs this town for the Commodore while he's away. And the Commodore's always away. As a matter of fact, I've never seen him."

"This knife doesn't cut!" complains Olive.

"Here, take mine," says Nana.

"Not since I was a child have we had a sharp knife in this house!" Olive declares.

Cole screams, "You owe me an apology! If you don't like our knives ... Bluto's rich, he can buy you lots of knives!"

"Please pass what's left," Wimpy calmly asks.

"I hate this table. It's ugly, and I'm the only one with nerve enough to tell the truth about it!"

The food gone, everyone begins leaving the table. Castor shouts, "Well, ask Bluto the pushover to buy you a new table!"

"Well, nothing's left," moans Wimpy.

"Bluto, Bluto, Bluto! Everyone takes advantage of my poor Bluto. Get a new glass! A new knife! Now they want a table!"

"That's why I always have to break off our engagement. To stop all you from taking advantage of the sweetest, most humble man on the face of the earth!"

"Well, it's never good to be too full, ya know."

L.ater.

"It's nine o'clock! Curfew! Lights out!"

But one light remains lit.

"Hello, Poppa. Soon you an' me, we'll be togedder. Thirty years ain't dat long!
Besides, nex Wednesday's our annualversity."

"So you want trouble, eh?"

"Stay alive. Dat's all I ax."

"Good night, Pap."

"I'll find ya!"

"Hrmph!!"

The next morning, Sweethaven's chapel bell
summons the townspeople to services.

But suddenly, music from the Roughhouse Cafe all but drowns out the bell's peal. The would-be worshippers are lured from the chapel path as Roughhouse begins his song.

"Everything is food, food, food."

"Everything is food to go."

"Everything is food for thought. Everything you knead is dough."

"It is food. Everything is food."

"Everything is
meat, meat, meat."

"Careful what you
put on your feet."

"Once it lived
on an annimul."

"Now it walks along with you.
It could be food."

"So throw some lettuce on it!"

"Food, food, food."

"And some tomato ketchup."

"Food, food, food.
Everything is food."

Wimpy fantasizes.
"I can just imagine a strawberry shortcake with a hamburger on the side. Or a banana split with a hamburger on the side!"

"Or even a hamburger with a hamburger on the side!"

"Or better still, a plain bread sandwich, which is one slice of bread between two hamburger paties. I love it! I love it!"

"Everything is upside down now.
Everything is sunny side up."

It's ubiquitous,
Enigmatic,
And"

"They can't trick us
With no hot dogmatic."

"It is food, food, food.
And it's full of flavor.
Food, food, food.
It's so good to savor."

"I would gladly pay you Tuesday
For a hamburger today."

"You didn't pay me Thursday for
what you ate yesterday."

"Everything is food, food, food. Everything is upside down. Everything is sunnyside up."

"It's ubiquitous."

"Enigmatic."

"And they can't trick us
With no hot dogmatic."

"It's food, food, food.
Make no mistake about it.
Food, food, food."

"Never ever doubt it.
Food, food, food.
Everything is food!"

"You owe me an apology!"
"Sorry, Pop."

"You know, there's a fifteen-cent Making-A-Mess Tax!"
"I didn't do it. Pop did it."

"Well, I'll only give you a warning this time. By the way, Mr. Oyl, how's your beautiful daughter?"

Popeye sits oblivious
to his surroundings.
"Oh, me Pap, me Pap!"
he mutters.

"Well! Whattaya have?"

"Gimme a burger rare."
"Burn one!"

"Me Pap,
me Pap.
Oh, me Pap!"

"That's a seven-cent
Melancholia Tax.
And that's an
additional three-cent
Mumbling Tax.
Ten cents!"

"Here.
Damn too
many taxes!
Take a hike!"

Spying Popeye's hamburger, Wimpy flits over to him like a fly to sugar and bursts into song:

*"What if I could read
What's on your mind,
Wouldn't you say,
There's a friend of mine?"*

*"And wouldn't you
Prepare yourself to pay?"*

"Through the nose, I hope!"

*"One who would explain
The things
You'd really like to say
Hey, hey."*

"Like younger,
I could explain that
Hunger,
It's just a state of mind."

"Why I could go for days
And days
Whilst never asking any praise."

"If I could only raise enough
To satisfy a sea that's rough,
And help a stranger
In his need."

"Who'll help me
Cultivate a need,
And sow the seed
Into my need."

"Everybody's got to eat!"

"I'll be right back."

"Sometimes a stranger
Can seem like a lender
Safe, compassionate
And wise."

"Ketchup?"

"When the going gets tough
And the journey gets rough,
Prepare yourself
For a big surprise."

"Mustard is nice."

"When it hurts too much to laugh,"

"And when you're much too old to cry."

"You must never tempt
The hand of fate.
And here's the reason why …"

"Everybody's got to eat."

"Everybody's got to eat."

"Boy, ye're right!" says Popeye. I needed someone t' talk t' fer a long time. Da jisk o' me story is I yam lookin' fer me Poppa. I yam searchin' da sevink seas. When I wuz about two, me own Pap leaves me. I ain't gonna cask no aspershkins, but me own Pap, he ditches me.

HA-HA-HA!

"I yam a very tolerink man, except when I holds a grudge. An' then I ain't so tolerink. I didn't t'ink I wud ever fergive me Pap, but sevink years ago I shipped · out on da *Gloomy Gus*. Kind of a depressin' boat, but dat's anudder story!"

HA-HA!

"It ain't dat funny!"

"We was carryin' hemp, an' we broke up off Guam in a typhloon. Dat's where da wind don't blow, ik sucks!"

"So's I wuz alone at sea on da rafk. Forty-five days out, widdout food er water but fer a coupla sharks an' sea gulls I caught. An' rain water. Boy, if I didn't have any water, I'd be a prune b'now!"

"After all dis time, I got a visitashikin, an' the visitashikin looks jus like me mudder, rest her soul...."

"An' she tol me dat me Pap wuz still alive ..."

"An' thirty years of a grudge is enuf, udderwise ya rots inside."

"So I been lookin' t' tell me Poppa I fergives 'im. I gotta fergive me Pap!"

"I'm on'y afeared he'll be dead by da time I finds him, and ik'll be too late fer 'im t' know wot a fine figger of a orphink I growed up into, widdout one whit o' his help wotsomuchasever."

"Hey!" shouts Spike. "You sure got a really nice-lookin' face, one eye!"

"I've seen better arms on a baboon!" adds Slug.
"You're a slimy lookin' shrimp!" taunts Mort.

As the cafe prepares for a battle, Butch shouts, "If you wants to know why you're lonksome, go take a look in the mirror!"

"Ya know, if dere's one t'ing I got, ik is a sensk o' humor."

"Where'd you get that pronunskiation?" snarls Mort.

"Did an olive get caught in your throat!"

"Ha, ha, har! I can enjoy a good laugh at meself."

"Now as I wuz sayin', me Pappy shipped out. ..."

But the taunts continue. "If I was your old man, I'd probably ship out too!" hollers Butch.

"Yeah," agrees Slug. "He's too dumb lookin' to leave on a doorstep!"

"Hey, runt!
I bet your
Poppa's as
ugly as
you are!"

"Anudder t'ing
I got is a sensk
of humiligration.
Now maybe ya
all cud pool yer
intelligenks an'
realize dat I's askin'
fer an apoligiky!"

"Butch, why don't you give daddy's boy an apology?" "With pleasure, Spike."

"The one-eyed rat wants an apology!"

"I would like to offer my most humfelt and sincere apologies!"

"Now you
apologize!"

"Now how about an apology for the little creep."   "I offer my most florid apologies and a free shave."

"Dis issa smorgasbork o' violence!"

"You apologize!"
"For what?"

"Well, that's everybody!"

"Now it's your turn to be sorry!"

"Well, I's really sorry I have t' do dis!"

WHUMP!

OOOOOH!

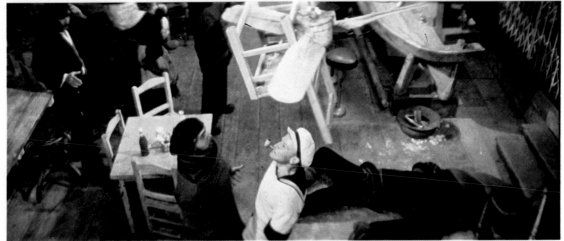

"Sorry!"

That evening most of Sweethaven turns out for the party celebrating Olive Oyl's engagement to Bluto. A good time is being had by all.

Then Popeye arrives ...   **and the party falls strangely silent.**

"Oh, Mr. Oyl! Wot's news?"

"Hmmm. It is kinda depressin', what with the price of whale oil."

"Well, I dunno when I's had dis much fun an' still been conscious!"

"Well, I'm gonna b' on me way. We gotta get togedder an' do dis more often."

"Like when eels grow legs, I guess!"

"Lovely party! I's jus goin' fer a lil' walk.

Meanwhile, Olive is dressing:

Mona Walfleur calls out. "Olive, look at this hat!"

"Ugly!" gasps Olive.

The Walfleur sisters speak in unison. "Bluto's ugly all right!"

"The hat's ugly!" says Olive. "Bluto's distinguished."

"Distinguishedly ugly!" say the sisters.

Olive pleads.
"Bluto's special!"
The Walfleurs titter.
"He's special all right.
Especially ugly!"

Olive continues dressing and begins to sing:

*"He's tall,
Good'lookin'
And
He's large."*

"Large!"

"Tall.
And large,
So large."

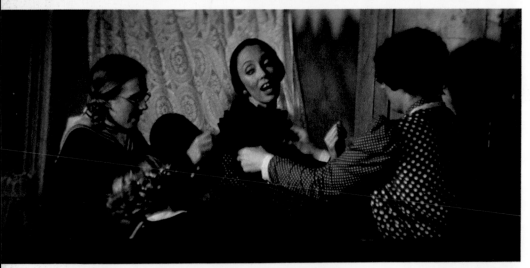

"And he's mine!"

"He's not a mandolin.
Oh, no!
He's an accordion.
I'll have to squeeze
him each night.
Ahhohhh!"

"He's virile,
And he's strong.
Strong!
And he's large."

While the Walfleurs aren't looking, Olive packs.

"*Do do,
Da do do.*"

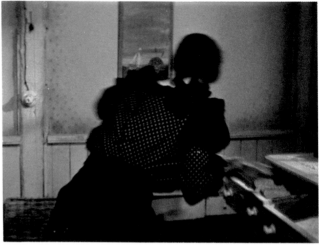

"*Da do do,
Da do da da dahhhh.*"

"*Da da dahhh!
Da da dahhh!*"

"*He's got money and respect.
He's better than the rest.
He may not be the best,
But he's large!*"
"*And he's mine!*"

Bluto arrives.

"Mother!"

"You got
my flowers?"

"Here's your
wife."

"Mrs. Oyl,
Olive is ...!"

"Olive's
what?"

"Olive's
getting
ready!"

At that moment ...

Olive is
backing out
of town.

OOOOOOH!

"What right have you to lurk here in the dark in the middle of the night and scare the wits out of a person!"

"How's da party?"

"That's a dumb question!" shrieks Olive.

"Where do you think I'm headed right this minute?"

"Well — ah — out o' town," suggests Popeye.

"Ohhh!
Thank you."

"I'm not headed
out of town!"
"Ya need help
wit yer bags?"
"No!"

"Oh! Oh! No,
that's the
wrong way!"

"She says ik's
da wrong way
so ik musk be
da wrong way!"
Popeye mutters.
"I want to go ...
that way,"
Olive points.

"Nooo!
That way!"

"Wait! That will
be a fifty-cent
Impersonating-A-Traffic-Cop
Tax."

"What!" shouts Olive.

"Oh, sorry, Miss Oyl,"
says the Taxman.

"I didn't recognize
you from behind."

"How come Miz Oyl
don't pay tax?"

"That's a ten-cent
Question Tax, but
I'll let you off
this time because
you're with Miss Oyl.
Good night."

"You think everyone pays taxes but me and my family. Don't you? Well, you couldn't be more wrong! You think it's because I'm engaged to Bluto and Bluto runs the town for the Commodore, we get special favors. Well, it's a lie!"

"Bluto's kind and generous and likes to do things for his loved ones. And you want me to hurt his feelings! Well, phooey on you! You don't even think enough of me to be at my engagement party!"

"And what are you doing here in Sweethaven anyway?"
"Lookin' fer me Pap."

"Well, if that's true, where is he?"
"I don't know, but I got a sensk dat he's here."

"Well, all right, I'll wait.

"What time will he be here?"
"Ah, soon."

Meanwhile Bluto also waits:

GGRRRRR!

"Here's a nice cup of tea for you, Captain Bluto."

CRUNCH!

"Where's Olive?"
"Olive? Oh! My daughter! She's ..."

CRACKLE!

CRUNCH!

"Oh, my stars and teacups!"

Still later:

"I remember me Pap. He used t' t'row me up in da air. But he wud never be dere when I came down."

"He has a funny sensk o' humor. He wud bounce me on his knee, an' he wud always misk."

As Popeye continues talking, a woman with a basket slinks down the staircase.

"He give me a electric eel once."

"Oh, me Pap. I figgered ik's becuz he wuz lookin' fer me, an' wit him lookin' an' me lookin', we misked each udder'."

"Seems like one o' us is always lookin' an' one is always waitin'."

"I waited a year in Singypore. An' I waited a year in Honorolulu …"

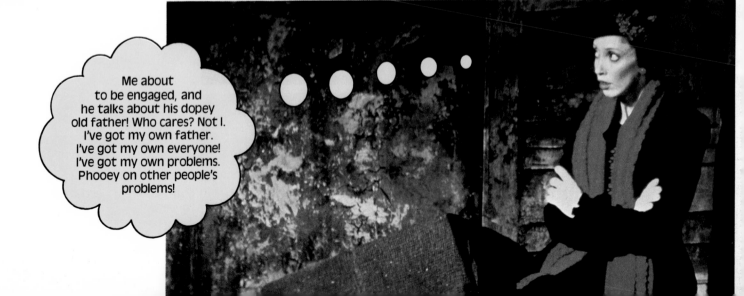

"... an' da year before dat I waited in Pago-Pago. A day in Samaki, a year in Bora-Bora, but dat wuz kinda borin' ..."

"Well, I'm not waiting any longer! I'm going to my engagement party now!"

"Oh, well, I wuz jus philosofizin'."

"What are you doing with that basket? It's not my basket!"

"Someone has deliberately painted that basket to look like my basket! My basket is clean and beautiful. This basket is ugly ..."

"Yipes! A rattlesnake! A rattlesnake!"

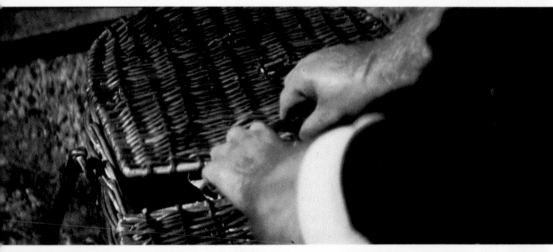

"Where issa rattlesnake? I'll rattle dat snake 'til ik wishked ik wuz a pair o' shoes!"

"What da!"

"Hmmm, a note. 'To da one-eyed sailor. I musk trusk someone wit me baby until I frees meself o' certain finanskal obligationks, which will take twenty-five years or so, at which time I shall reclaim him. Inna meantime, love him as only a mudder cud.' Signed 'A Mudder.'"

"Ahhh!"

Back at the Oyl house, Bluto's patience is at an end:

"WHERE'S OLIVE!!!"

CRASH!

"WHERE'S MY OLIVE!!!"

At that moment:

"Coochie, coochie, coo!"

"Boy, when ya t'rows a party, ya t'rows a party!" Popeye exclaims.

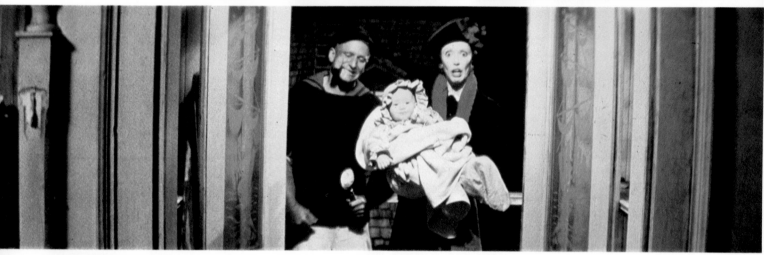

Bluto sees red.

GGRRRRR!

"Ik's a logical misunderstandink! I'd make da same mistake meself! I knows what yer t'inkin'..."

But Bluto is in no mood for talk!

SLAM!

THUD!

SPLASH!

"Don't t'inks
I blames ya,
'cause I
doesn't!"

"Here, d' ya wants me pipe?" asks Popeye.

"Oh! You're doing it all wrong! You'll hurt her!" shouts Olive.

"A lot you knows!" Popeye snaps back. "Her issa him!"

Popeye sighs. "He's me lil' Swee'pea."

"Sweetpea!" Olive shrieks. "You're bats!"

Popeye is indignant. "I found him in Swee'having, so he is me Swee'pea! I yam callin' him Swee'pea. Dat is his name!"

Olive counters. "That's the worst name I ever heard for a baby!"

"Yeah?" says Popeye. "Wot does you wants t' call him? Baby Oyl?"

Meanwhile Olive's broken engagement to Bluto has had dire financial consequences for the Oyl family.

The Taxman reads a list of taxes now levied against the family.
"Whereas you are in arrears on your household and appurtenances maintenance tax, by order of the authority vested in me by Captain Bluto on behalf of his Honor, the Commodore, you owe the sum of twelve-thousand, twelve-hundred, twelve-dollars, and twelve cents!"

Then opportunity knocks.

And Caster decides to answer.

What could happen to me? Well, I could get killed. It would be worth getting killed to help Mom and Pop! What if I won? I'm fast. I'm foxy. I'm going to be rich and loved and famous and feared. Maybe even the Commodore will see me!

"Nuttin like a good fight t' takes yer mind off yer troubles. Fights is fun!"

"Oh! Fights aren't fun!"

DING!

DING!

"Ladies and gentlemen! Citizens of Sweethaven! His Honor the Commodore invites you to risk life and limb for ten golden days of tax exemption and fifteen dollars in hard cash for you or your next of kin!"

"What martyr in our midst will be the first to attempt to last one scandalous round with that ugliest of plug-uglies, that unworthiest of unworthies, that pejorative of pugilism, Oxblood Oxheart?"

As Popeye and the Oyl family get seated, Castor bounds into the ring.

Nana suddenly shouts, "Olive, you've got to get your brother out of there!"

But alas, it is too late.
"Gentlemen, you know the rules. The rules are that there are no rules. This is a fight to the finish. And may the best man win."

The bell sounds and, of course, Castor is no match for Oxheart.

POW!

THUMP!

KICK!

Oxheart's kick sends the battered Castor sailing from the ring.

WHOOSH!!

Annoyed by Oxheart's lack of sportsmanship, Popeye shouts, "I'll teaches ya how t' fight fair!" and jumps into the ring.

"Oooo, Popeye! You can't do that! You'll be murdered!"

DING!

DING!

"This one looks easy, Mom."

"All right, gentlemen. This is a fight to the finish. So let's come out fighting."

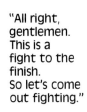

Magically, Sweetpea reassures a worried Olive.

"He'll be okay?" asks Olive.

"Weeeeeeeeeeeee!"

"He'll win?"

"Weeeeeeeeeeeee!"

"He won! He won! You were right! I don't know how you knew, but you knew! Let's go see Popeye."

The next day:

"Well, after taxkes ik don't come t' much!"

"The main thing," says Olive, "Is that you're all right."

"'Dja t'ink he'd kill me or somethink?"

"Oh, Popeye! Don't be silly. I knew after I asked Sweetpea!"

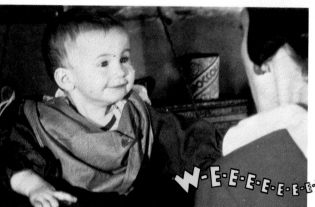

"I asked Sweetpea, and he told me. Didn't you, Sweetpea?"

"Wuzzat?"

"Wotta ya know! Swee'pea, me son da profik!" exclaims Popeye as Wimpy becomes suddenly interested.

Cole remarks, "That kid is a regular forecaster. Remind me to talk to him about gold futures!"

"I am interested in talking to him about more immediate futures!" mumbles Wimpy.

"Oh, Popeye! This adorable little fellow looks a bit peaked. He needs some air. With your permission I'll take him for a walk."

"O' courske!" agrees Popeye. "After all, ya is like his uncle."

"I wanted to take him for a walk!"

"Oh, leaves him be wit Uncle Wimpy, Olives!"

"Oh, Wimpy can take him, but I can't!"

"Who says ya can't?

"You said I can't!"

"Dat wuz before."

"Before what?"

"Before I knew ya wuz worried 'bout me."

"You mean now I can hold him because I was worried about you?"

"Yeah!"

"Phooey!"
"Ya sez phooey t' me?"
"I said phooey and
I mean phooey!"

"Phooey!"

Meanwhile Wimpy is taking Sweetpea for more than just a walk.

Over an hour has passed.

"Where is he? Where is he?"

"I don't see them anywhere!" worries Olive. "Maybe they went to the Roughhouse," says Cole.

"Oh, my stars and horses!" exclaims Nana. "Derby Day!" shouts Olive.

"Wot's dis got t' do wit me Swee'pea?" asks Popeye. "They've gone to the races!" shouts Cole.

"Where is dese races?" screams Popeye. "C'mon, let's go!" screeches Olive.

Later at the casino

Bluto watches what's been happening with interest.

"C'mon! C'mon!"

"And the winner is Cat's Pajamas!"

"Yipee! You did it, Sweetpea!
We won again!"

As Wimpy is collecting his winnings, Popeye and the Oyls arrive.

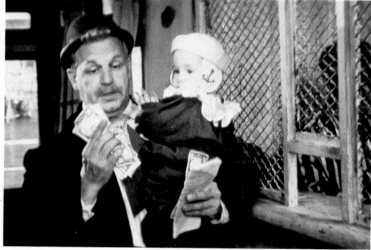

"Dere he is! I yam disgustipated! I feels like sockin' 'im inna mush!"

Popeye grabs Sweetpea.

"What's this?" asks Olive as she grabs Wimpy's money.

"One-hundred-and-twenty Semolians!" sputters Wimpy.

"Really! Disgraceful! How many races?"

"Three."

"Hmm, let me see that racing form!" Olive demands.
Popeye is indignant.

"No chilt o' mine is goin' t' be a racin' trout!"

"Now wait a minute! Sweetpea! How about Osteopath? Cold Comfort? Sucking Lemons?"

"Me chilt will not be exploitikated fer ill-gotten games!"

"It's not ill-gotten! It's good-gotten. These gains will feed us and clothe us and save us!" screams Olive as she grabs Sweetpea from Popeye.

"Sweetpea says it'll be Sucking Lemons. One-hundred-and-twenty Semolians on Sucking Lemons!"

A disappointed Popeye begins to sing.

"What am I?
Some kind o' barnacle
On da dinghy o' life?"

"I ain't no doctor,
But I knows when I'm
Loosin' me patience."

"Then wot am I?
Some kind o' judge?
Or lawyer?
Maybe not,
But I knows
wot suits me."

"So wot am I?
I ain't no
psykiakerisk,
But I knows
wot matters."

"What am I?"

"I'm Popeye da Sailor!"

"And I yam wot I yam wot I yam! And I yam wot I yam. And that's all dot I yam!"

"'Cause I yam wot I yam!"

"Ya got it?
Yah, I think so!"

*"And I got a lot o' muskle.
And I only got one eye.
And I never hurt nobody.
And I never tell a lie."*

*"From me top t' me bottom,
From me bottom t' me top.
That's da way it is,
Till the day dat I drop."*

*"Wot am I?
I yam wot I yam!"*

"I yam wot I yam."

"What I yam,
What I yam,
What I yam."

"I can open up an ocean.
I can lose a lotta sail.
I can take a lotta water,
And I've never had t' bail.
Off the coast of Madagascar,
Grabbed a whale by da tail!"

"Wot am I?
Wot am I?"

"I YAM WOT I YAM!"

*"I'm Popeye
the Sailor!"*

*"I'm Popeye
the Sailor!"*

*"I yam wot I yam,
And dat's all dat I yam."*

*"I am wot I yam,
Wot I yam, wot I yam.*

*"I'M POPEYE
DA SAILOR MAN!"*

And Bluto hatches his plan.

Early the
next day:

"I hate t' do
dis, but ik's
neckessary."

Nana cries out.
"Oh, it's cruel,
Mr. Eye!
Er … Mr. Pop.
Er … Mr. Eyepop."

Popeye is firm.
"I yam sorry, Miz Oyl,
but a fodder
gotta duty t' pertek
his orphink from
chilt abusk."

Nana pleads.
"But think of Olive!
You can't take
that poor baby
away from poor
Olive!"

"Moraliky ain't
doughnuts!
Me mind is set!
An' when me mind
is set, I don't
t'ink o' nuttin."

"Oh, my stars and fathers!" exclaims Nana.
"Maybe we owe him an apology!" adds Cole.

Later Popeye settles into his new home — a corner of the lumber mill.

"You'll fergive me fer dis one day. I know ya will. You'll grow up t' be a strong perskin."

"Ik ain't no manger, but ik'll do.
I luv ya so like you'll never know!"

Suddenly the Taxman appears.
"You moved out of the Oyls?"
"None o' yer buzniss!"
"Four dollars and twenty-five cents Moving-Out Tax."
"Gnat's t' ya! An' gnats t' yer taxkes, too!"

"You moved in here?"
"Wot's ik look like?"
"Five dollars and twenty-five cents Moving-In Tax."
"Double gnats!"

"Where did this baby come from?"
"Da pelican brought him."
"Eighty-nine cents Unlicensed-Baby Tax."

"Why don't ya go take a hike!"

**Suddenly the townspeople run into the streets, jumping for joy.
Popeye becomes an instant hero.**

"Hooray! Hooray!"

"Hooray! Hooray!"

"Where's Swee'pea?"

"Swee'pea! Swee'pea!"

Wimpy talks to himself.
"This can't be me.
Not J. Wellington Wimpy.
Someone else is doing this.
One of the Jones Boys
is doing this! Jones,
you are beneath contempt!
Don't speak to me!"

"Gimme the kid!"

"I won't! But Jones
will. He has no
conscience."

"Here's your thirty hamburgers.
Now gimme the kid!"

"You mention this to anybody, and
I'll feed you to the sharks!"

"Jones, you
are despicable!
Despicable
but hungry."

Hours pass.
Night falls.

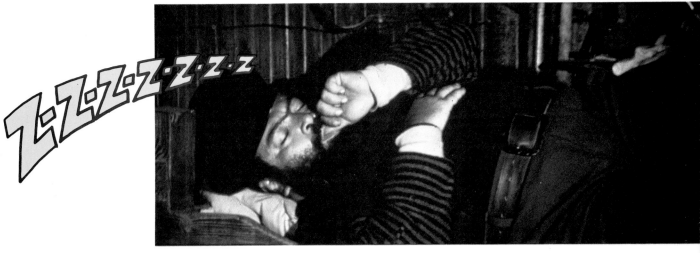

Z·Z·Z·Z·Z·Z·Z

At the lumber mill, Popeye mutters his thoughts to himself.

"A man's supposed t' stand alone sometimes, especially if he looks like me. I'm used t' standin' alone."

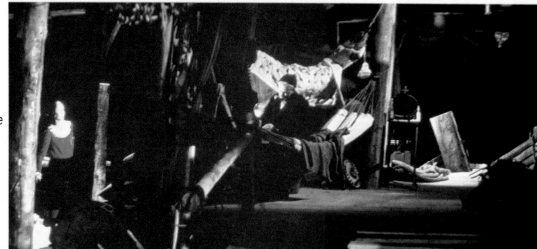

"I wishk I cud send up a flare 'cause sometimes I gets da feelin' I needs somebody."

"I lost me momma when I wuz born. I lost me Paps when I wuz two. Now I lost me Swee'pea. An' even though I never had her, I lost me Olive, too."

Olive's heart leaps as she whispers, "He needs me!"

The next day.

"Ah-hah! Bluto and Sweetpea!"

Olive screams. "What did you say about Sweetpea?"

A startled Wimpy lies, "Er ... I said nothing!"

But then relents. "Ohhhh, I confess! I turned him over to Bluto, who's taking him to the Commodore's boat.

"You what?!" screeches Olive. "Oh, that rat Bluto! I gotta go!"

"Miss Oyl! Wait! I'll go with you!"

Moments later.

"Nobody goes on the Commodore's boat but the Commodore," pants Wimpy as he struggles to keep up with Olive.

"What's the matter? Don't you have any gumption?" answers an angry Olive.

"Wimpy, open that door!"

"I'm sure there's nobody home!"

"Open that door, Wimpy. Or do I have to kick you?"

"I'm opening it, I'm opening it!"

As Olive steps through the doorway, she hears a familiar voice.

"Infinks! I hates infinks!"

"Hatin's me code! I will live an' die by hate!"

"Hates dun me more good dan ant'ing else in da werld!"

"Eat yer spinach, ya no-good infink!"

Bluto growls. "Commodore! ..."

"Shhhhhhh!"

"Don't go callin' me Commodore inside this here harbor. I got millions o' enemies, and yer ten or twelve of 'em!"

"What a good, no-good infink. See how he eats his spinach."

"I call you an old fool!" Bluto booms. "We can break the bank at the betting parlor. This kid can predict the future!"

"Look, he's got Popeye's arms!"

"I don't wanna break the bank inna bettin' parlor, ya non-entiky. I owns the bettin' parlor! An' I owns you! An' don't talk t' me 'bout no future. I hates the future. And I hates the past. And I hates the presenk! Especkally you!"

"Look! He's got Popeye's arms. Popeye's eye! We better tell Popeye we found them. Let's go!"

"All these years I've been loyally mean, and all these years you drop hints of buried treasure! You think that's fair!"

"Don't say I ain't fair! True, I hates, but I come by my hatin' fair n' square!"

"Ten years of waiting, you old goat! Taking orders! Taking abuse! Bidding my time. Well, if this kid isn't your fortune, he's mine!"

"Grrrrr!
I hate you
so much!"

"Dadblast ya! Dadblast ya!
Dablasted blasted! Untie me!"

"Untie me an' I'll kill ya!"

"Untie me an' I'll eat yer heart out!"

"Untie me an' I'll make ya rue
the day ya untied me!"

"Untie you! Will you lead me to your treasure?"
"What treasure? I lied, Lies!"

"Kid, is the old goat holding out on me?
"Weeeeeeeeeeee!"

"Now, kid, listen. This is the crucial question. Can
you lead me to the old goat's treasure?"

"Don't tell him! Don't tell him! Ya little rat-fink
infink!"

"Ha, ha, ha, ha, ha!"

Olive and Wimpy run to tell Popeye that they've found Sweetpea, Bluto, and the Commodore.

"And what's more," says Wimpy, "It appears that your father is the Commodore!"

"He ain't no hoity-toity Commodore!" shouts Popeye. "He's a rat, a crook, a kidnapper, a bad father, and a Commodore!" snaps Olive.

Popeye storms off to prove them wrong.

The townspeople get wind of what's going on and follow.

But only so far.

"Me Paps. I knows he's in here. No, he ain't! But wot if he is?"

"What? Who? Somebody comin' t' see me?"

"All right! I knows ya ain't down here.
An' if ya is, den ya ain't him!"

"So where ain't ya, an' where ain't me Swee'pea?"

As Bluto creeps out with Sweetpea, Popeye comes face to face with the Commodore.

"Poppa?"

"I ain't nobody's Poppa, ya one-eyed, fish-faced, sissipated, sniffle-snaffle! I yam Poppa t' no male ner female chilt dat no court cud prove udderwise!"

"Poppa! Pap! Ik's me, yer orphink son!"

"I hates senktiment! I yam disgustipated! Gnats to you! Phooey!"

"Stand to, ya swab! Yer caskin' shadows on Poopdeck Pappy, pride o' da Paciferic an' fodder t' the shark, brudder t' da piranika, an' uncle t' da oktapussy!"

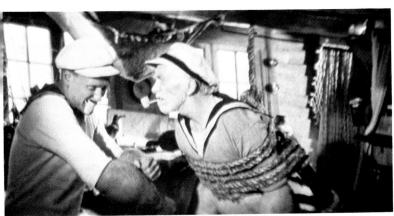 

"But Poppa! I yam yer one an' only exprang! Lookit, da same bulgy arms!"

"No resemblinks!"

"We got da same squinky eye!"

"Wot squinky eye? No resemblinks!"

"We got da same pipe, Pap!"

"Ya idgit! Ya can't inherit a pipe! Dere's on'y one way t' prove I ain't yer fodder. Pick up dat can o' spinach!"

"Pick it up! Bring it here an' eat it!" the Commodore commands.

"Eat ik?"
"Eat it!"
"Raw?"
"Raw!"

"I don't wan' no spinach! I hates spinach! I don't wanna eat ik!"

"You eat it, you brat!"

"Disobedienk at two
an' disobedienk now!
Ya wudn't eat yer
spinach. Spinach!
Wot kept our fambly strong
fer t'ousins o' yers!
An' wot does me on'y
exprang do? He spits it up!"

"His mudder ups 'n dies, an'
he wudn't eat his spinach!
His Poppa outta woik, an' he
wudn't eat his spinach!
Da whole country inna
depreshkin, an' he wudn't eat
his spinach!"

"His Poppa goin' hungary!
Goin' out t' steal! Stealin'
wot? Spinach! So his ungrate
son cud grow up big
an' strong!"

"Eat dat dadblasted spinach
and cut me down!"

"He's gettin' away! He's
gettin' away wit dat lil' infink
of a stool pigeon, an' he's
goin' t' fine me treasure! Let's
get outta here!"

Meanwhile.

"Come back here, Bluto!"

"Unhand me, you brute!"

"This does it, Bluto! This takes the cake! I hope you realize we're finished!"

Within moments the Commodore runs to his boat. "After da swine! All hands on deck!"

"Olive!"

"Help! Oh!"

"Ha, ha, har! You'll never catch me!" Bluto yelps as he steers the *Vile Body* to sea.

"Help! Popeye, save us!" "I'm comin', Olive!"

"Is that where the treasure is?" questions Bluto. Sweetpea answers affirmatively. "Weeeeeeeeeee!"

An hour later. The *Vile Body* is out of sight.

Popeye despairs. "We ain't never gonna fine 'em."

Suddenly Castor shouts, "Look! There he is! We found them!"

"Scab Island? Dat's where me treasure is hidden. Dat dirty bilge rat! He's not gonna get away wit dis! You! You wit da crazy beard an' da fat guy! Come up here! Move it, move it, I want ya t' move dis cannon!"

Popeye is concerned. "Pap! Wot're ya doin'? Ya can't fire! Me Olive an' me Swee'pea is on dat boat!"

"Don't ya worry. I ain't gonna hit 'em! I's jus firin' a warnin' shot! Don't ya t'ink I know what I'm doin'?"

"Now look out!"

Carried away by the taste of victory, the Commodore orders, "Full speed ahead!"

Dismayed, Popeye shouts, "Full speed ahead? Hows will we be able t' board her?"

"We're not gonna board her! I'm gonna ram it! He can't get away wit me treasure!"

As the boat speeds up, Popeye is frantic. "Ya can't ram ik! Wot about Olive an' me Swee'pea?"

The Commodore is single-minded. "I don't care about them! All I cares about is me treasure!"

"Abandon ship! Abandon ship!"

Meanwhile.

"Ha, ha, haaa! Pirate's Cove! I should have known!"

"I'll have you know that my brother Castor is pretty good with a bow and arrow! And other medieval weapons! Like boiling oil! Crossbones! Hemlock!"

"He's not going to forget this! I'll make sure of that! And I'll never get engaged to you again!"

Bluto ignores Olive. "Kid, we're gonna be rich. At least, I am! You wait here while I go get the treasure."

Olive screeches.
"Wait a minute! Where do you think you're going?"

Suddenly.

"Popeye!"

"You little runt!"

"Bluto, ya may be bigger dan me, but ya can't win 'cause yer bad! And ya knows good always wins over bad!"

"Oh, yeah!"

R-R-R-R-R-R

"Bluto!
Here
I is!"

"Now ya see me ..."

"... now ya don't!"

"That's it, Popeye! Hide! You'll never find him, Bluto!"

"Where are you?
I'm gonna eat you
for breakfast!"

"Here I am! Come an' get it!"

At the same time, the Commodore and his water-logged crew manage to reach the cove.

"Get up here, you undertaker! Move it! I need help wit me treasure!"

"Ah-ha! There it is! There it is!"

"Grab that rope! I gotta get me treasure!"

Meanwhile the fight continues.

"I think
we owe
him an
apology!"

And to complicate matters even more, a sea creature has its eye on Sweetpea.

As the Commodore concentrates on his treasure …

… and Popeye concentrates on surviving …

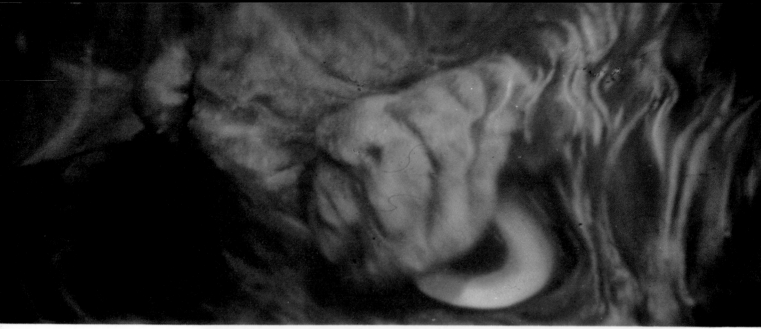

... the creature
concentrates
on Sweetpea.

And the fight continues.

"Grrrrrrr!"

Cole tries to help. "Popeye! Here's a sword!"

"Dat ain't fair!" shouts a bewildered Popeye.

"So ya need a sword, ya runt!"

SWISH!

At that moment.

Popeye
and Bluto
are still
at it.

"Here I yam!"

"Grrr!
The next hole
in you I'm
gonna make!"

"Popeye!"

"Hey! Hey! Dere's an oktapussy down dere! He's goin' t' get da kid! Get over her an' help me!

"We gotta get dat kid! Dat rotten infink!"
"Stay where ya are! I'm goin' t' save ya!"

"I gots t' hook 'im!"

"Okay, now pull!"

"Okay, ya rotten infink, I got ya now!"

"Ya rotten infink!
I saved ya life!
Ya guys be careful.
Don't drops dat kid
or I'll kills ya!"

Popeye and Bluto battle ...

... as the octopus goes for Olive.

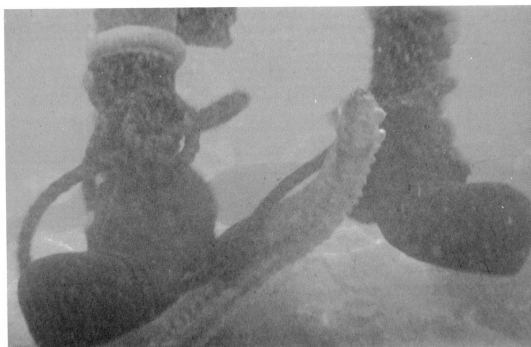

And the Commodore unveils his treasure.

"Now, kid, you're gonna see somethin' no one's ever seen. Me treasure!"

"Here it is!"

"Dese is Popeye's shoes!"

"Here's his spinach."

"And ... ohhhh! Ahhh!"

Popeye and Bluto carry on.

"Grrrrrrr!"

"Ya gotta eat spinach!"

Meanwhile

"Ohhhh, help! Popeye! Octopus! Octopus!"

BAM!

SPLASH!

GURGLE!

Olive wrestles the octopus.

The Commodore shouts ...

"Ya sissipated sniffle-snaffle! If ya wudda eats yer spinach, ya wudn't be losin' dis fight!"

... as Popeye wrestles Bluto.

"I ain't gonna eat no spinach!"

"An' I ain't losin'! No, I ain't"

"Ya disobedienk brat! Here! Eat yer spinach!"

"Ha, ha! Bull's-eye!"

Popeye screams.
"I don't wan' spinach! I yam not gonna eat ik!"

Bluto growls.
"So you don't like it, eh?"

"Well, now you're gonna eat it!"

"See ya in Davey Jones's locker, sucker!"

"Now, my treasure!"

"Oh, Popeye! My hero!"

"Look at him swim!"   "Swim! You 400-pound canary!"

*"I'm Popeye
the Sailor Man."*

*"I'm Popeye
the Sailor Man!"*

*"I'm strong t' the finich,
'Cause I eats me spinach.
I'm Popeye the Sailor Man!"*

*"He's Popeye
the Sailor
Man."*

*"He's Popeye
the Sailor
Man!"*

*"He's strong
to the finich,
Because he eats
all his spinich."*

"He's Popeye
the Sailor Man!"

"I'm one tough gazookas,
Which hates all palookas
Wot ain't on the up an' square."

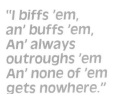

"I biffs 'em,
an' buffs 'em,
An' always
outroughs 'em
An' none of 'em
gets nowhere."

"If anyone dasses
ta risk me fisk,
It's boff an'
it's wham.
Unnerstan?"

"So keep
good behavor
That's yer
one lifesaver
With Popeye
the Sailor
Man."

"He's Popeye the Sailor Man."

"He's Popeye the Sailor Man."

"He's strong to the finish."

"Because he eats all his spinach."

*"He's Popeye
the Sailor
Man!"*